The Writing Marathon

From 9pm on November 17th to Midnight Nov 18th, 36 writers took part in an Internet Write-a-thon to support BBC's Children in Need.

The writers responded to prompts given to them via the Internet every hour.

The Write-a-thon was a great success and will raise almost £10,000 for the charity.

Leaf Books are proud to be publishing the best of the stories in this book.

About Leaf Books

Our mission is to provide readers with a pocket-sized read in the places where they are waiting, relaxing, taking a break. We aim to support writers by giving them a new market for their short stories and short non-fiction.

This book is produced jointly with a group of on-line writers led by Alex Keegan.

All profits will go to BBC Children in Need.

Visit our website at:

www.leafbooks.co.uk

for more information about this book and other services from Leaf Books.

Children in Need

Children in Need is a charity run by the BBC which raises money for children in the UK.

"BBC Children in Need helps disadvantaged children to have a better life. These include children who are chronically ill or profoundly disabled, those who've been badly treated by the adults around them, children who live in poverty or inadequate housing, and some who are bullied, excluded or distressed."

BBC Children in Need website
www. bbc.co.uk/pudsey

First published by Leaf Books Ltd in 2005

www.leafbooks.co.uk

Leaf
GTi Suite,
Valleys Innovation Centre,
Navigation Park,
Abercynon,
CF45 4SN

Leaf Books are proud to be working with
The University of Glamorgan

Printed and supported by Inka
www.inkagraphics.com
ISBN 1-905599-10-2
ISBN 978-1-905599-10-3

1,620 Minutes

Winning Stories from the 2005 Internet Writing Marathon

in aid of
BBC Children in Need

Contents

First Prize

Paper Crowns

Father is wearing a paper crown. He has a smile on his face that could not be removed for a suitcase full of hard cash.

Mother is in the kitchen. She is not wearing a paper crown. Daughter, who is wearing a paper crown, has tried to put one on Mother's head, but Mother blocked the approach with an armed arm. She looks at her daughter and apologises and puts the crown on her head. Daughter goes back into the sitting room and sees Son, who is unwrapping a game for his new console. Daughter tries to put a paper crown on Son's head but is waved away. Father smells trouble even through the fumes of brandy.

'Now Mark, let your sister put a paper crown on your head. And then we can read out our jokes,' says Father. With a grimace at his sister, Son puts the crown back on his head.

Father's paper crown is ringed with sweat. He reads a joke from a cracker.

'What do you call a man with a spade in his head?'…'Anyone? What do you call a man with a spade in his head?'

Perhaps Grandfather will know the answer to the joke. Grandfather is wearing a paper crown at an angle. He is sitting in his reserved armchair, unhappy because he can no longer see well enough to read, and he has a knee operation coming up, and he lost his wife thirteen years ago, and he has an upset stomach.

'Grandpa? What do you call a man with a spade in his head?'

Grandfather looks at his son-in-law. He hates being called Grandpa. Two men, thrown together in mutual loathing, neither giving a millimetre, praying for the day to end, both thinking about women not in the room.

'Come on, Grandpa,' says Daughter, who has recovered from her small trauma. She did not sleep the night before, due to excitement about this day. It is her seventh Christmas on

Earth. 'It's easy.'

'I don't know. Keith, I should think,' says Grandfather.

Daughter laughs. Father laughs and adjusts his crown.

'No, Doug! Doug, get it?'

He laughs again and picks up his glass. Grandfather's hands are folded across his cardigan. Now he is thinking about swimming. When he was a child he lived in the Isles of Scilly, and used to swim in the sea every morning before breakfast. It gave him a tremendous sense of perspective each day.

Mother comes in with a bowl of vegetables.

'I'm afraid these are burned. The oven isn't working. It should have been fixed. The electrician said it was fixed. It's not working. These are burned.'

'Don't worry, Mum,' says the daughter.

Mother found out about Father's affair two days before Christmas. Her mask slipped within a few hours of the discovery, and now it is on the floor next to her paper crown.

Son is playing a game where he controls an entire civilization. He is listening to a new i-pod and eating sweets while he plays. He is lying on his stomach. In the game, he is unleashing a terrible disease that kills millions of people around the world.

At some point in the afternoon, when everyone is full or sick, there are some moments of silence. The television has yet to be turned on. Inspired by brandy, Father looks across at Mother hopefully, and then looks down again at the table.

The winter sun moves in parallelograms across the room. Son wants to go outside and find an animal to kill. Daughter is playing with the toy in her cracker, a plastic doll's mirror. When Mother sees this, she thinks she won't be able to bear it any longer. Grandfather sees, and in a moment of purest inspiration, a moment of undiluted love for a daughter who is stuck with a caveman husband…Grandfather, without the love of his own life and no longer able to swim, feigns a choking fit. His eyes are squeezed shut as he coughs, the paper hat slipping further down his head but not falling off. Mother goes across, relieved to be given a focus for her concern, and Father goes into the kitchen for a glass of water. Son turns the TV on and Daughter carries on playing with her mirror.

After that the day is a little bit softer and cooler, although it still lasts years and years for Mother and Father. The day lasts just a few moments for Daughter, who will also never forget it, although it will change in her memory as she finds things out. Grandfather will forget it, although he will try and hang on to it, and Son will remember only dull rage.

Dave Prescott

Second Prize

Advice Never Received

A list of useful things
That your mother may have forgotten to tell you
(Get a cup of tea, we might be a while).

When crossing a lake
In a barrel
Don't read a funny book
(Life is a serious thing).
You will shake with laughter,
Roll around in the barrel,
Water will get inside and you'll sink.
We never taught you how to swim.

Dad's voice, offstage:
Make sure it's a lake you're crossing, son.
You don't want to sail into the Niagara.
If you survive the fall, they'll fine you.

When dressed in a giant, pink chicken

costume,
Patrolling the streets of Manhattan
With a leather briefcase under your left wing,
Address policemen respectfully.
They are only trying to do their job.
And when they hit you,
Meditate on Buddhist forgiveness.

Dad's voice, offstage:
Dress as a Hungarian three-legged chicken.
You'll be able to run faster
When they try to arrest you.
And if they still catch you
They won't understand what you're saying
And won't be able to use it against you in court.

When climbing a giant cactus
Wear light clothing and no gloves
(Life hurts and you should know that).
You are allowed to drink the water inside the cactus
To avoid sunstroke
But not too much

Or it will collapse underneath you.
And you've only ever flown in your dreams.

Dad's voice, offstage:
Bring your sailing certificate
And an insurance form.
If they commit you to an asylum
You can just claim that you were climbing the mast
To look out for wet land.

There is no more advice.
No more time for this lesson.
I lied when I said this would take a while.
Anyway
Your mother and father taught you enough.

Cedric Popa

Third Prize

Loo Seat in Disguise

Loo seat in disguise, with diamonds. Disguise? Disguise in love with you. This guy is.

There must be a hundred ways to fall stupidly in love. Like watching the way someone stands on one leg as they look at the paintings, their resting foot tucked neat behind and around the working ankle.

There must be a thousand ways to fall stupidly in love. Maybe this someone is wearing a purple hat that doesn't match the coat. What Not To Wear – How To Find My Heart. They clasp their hands behind them and you think: 'I could do that; I could save you the trouble of holding your own hands. Please.'

The million ways include watching the way they sway – just a little – on the working foot, so they can scan the painting. You can see their eyes drinking the colour.

One way not to is to stand too close, so they catch you with a glance and turn away, leaving you staring into space - as if they'd printed something in the air.

She's called Lucy. You know because her friend said it. And Lucy said, yes, she'd like a coffee. The tables are stainless steel, stained with coffee rings and bleached with milk. The chairs have steel bands that hug your back. The coffee is in a cafetiere and is 'how much?' expensive. I sound like my mum.

The friend is chatty, rolling stories out onto the table. Lucy scratches the tip of her nose and you think, again, 'I could do that.' When she laughs, she shows tiny teeth.

The best way to fall stupidly in love is to read the artist's catalogue. Hold it so the tops of the pages form a 'v' and sight it onto Lucy. Try looking at her with one eye, then the other.

The worst way is to watch how her eyelashes

dip as she blinks, a hesitation on the close like butterfly wings drinking sunshine. That's bad for the real heart; it makes it race like caffeine.

What if she comes across? Hands-in-pocket-out-of-pockets, shy. 'My friend says... she thinks...are you?' She ducks a head at the catalogue. A comma of hair slips from the purple hat and swings free. You can't help but think 'I'd like to paint with that. Make Lucy brushes.'

The only way to fall stupidly in love is to let the catalogue slip through your fingertips, because you forgot you were holding it, your brain otherwise occupied with thanking God. You'd awake to several senses breaking through at the same time: the spike-pain of hot coffee on your trouser leg; the high 'c' of the cafetiere finding the floor; the heady cloud of roasted Columbian coffee beans.

'Hi,' you'd say, a damp palm offered across

the remains. And you'd smile and say yes, you were, in a confident/shy way and ask her, and her friend of course, to visit your studio, maybe.

The very, very worst way would be to find some elf had super-glued your tongue to the roof of your mouth, so all you could do was wave your arms and make a noise that sounded, even to you, like 'loo seat, loo seat' and watch as Lucy walked away.

Henry Peplow

Low Fat Sex

Tonight I will scoop out pumpkins with my daughters. They will cut eyes, a nose and a mouth into the flesh, supervised, of course, and I will spread the seeds onto a baking tray and toast them lightly. I'll mix them with sunflower seeds and pine nuts to make a healthy snack.

Tom will come home and we will eat a supper of fresh pasta lightly dressed with a tomato-based sauce accompanied by a rocket and red basil salad (no dressing). When I'm stacking the dishwasher he'll come up behind me and kiss my neck and whisper in my ear. He'll tell me how great my arse looks. Two tight little buns hard enough to crack nuts with. (And you will, won't you, you little minx?)

Later we will go to bed (after showering) and have seven minutes of sex. Sex that doesn't mess up my hair or ruffle my sheets. We will sleep side by side without touching.

Tomorrow morning when I am eating fruit and natural yoghurt for breakfast I will blush as I remember dreaming about being ravished as I eat a bar of chocolate.

Janet Bradshaw

Doubt Comes on a Friday

Jack was so certain. Two and two is four, the sky is blue, Friday is fish fingers and he'll never get married to a girl.

You get the picture: he's five and God's in His heaven and every day is new and some days, hey, no, most days, I feel a little jealous of my son.

Pathetic isn't it? Time enough for doubt and low self esteem, give him his childhood - you know the clichés. Hell, I wrote the book.

But there comes a time when it all changes and fear rules a once fair world. It happened to me with my first wet dream; it just came earlier for Jack.

She died all of a sudden, just collapsed getting the fish fingers out of the oven. We never fried them. I was there and they all said that was a blessing, but I know, curse my eyes,

I know it made all the difference.

Nothing too dramatic: she just slid down the oven door and gave a little sigh. Didn't even bump her head on the way down. Graceful I suppose. Jay was always graceful.

'Mummy's slipped,' said Jack. I remember that, and he gave a little laugh. But for the first time, the very first time, there was a hint of something else in that laugh.

'Mummy, wake up,' he said and I'm thinking, curse me for the callous shit I am, oh come on, he must know she's not asleep. Watch carefully. This is your son losing his innocence; this is a day you'll remember.

My wife is lying dead on the kitchen tiles and I'm conducting an anthropological experiment, noting that the fish fingers are slightly overcooked, seeing that Jack is just starting to cry, thinking, bloody hell, this was unexpected.

And Jack turns and looks at me then; I mean

he looks at ME. And he sees, and he knows, and that's what breaks my heart, more than Jay dying and more than the trauma my son will live with forever. He sees the doubt and the fear and the cold, cold shield I hide behind. And he sees his life mapped out and he sees what he'll become and in that instant the light goes out of his eyes and I wish it was me lying on that floor.

Chris Bleach

The Life and Death of Bertram Wilson in 592 Words

The last line of this story is not what you want to hear but don't blame me. Well, actually, do blame me, but understand that I'm simply here to guide you through the last day of Bertram Wilson's life.

Bertram was an innocent, a boy from a different age; an Edwardian gentlechild with a baseball cap and a hoodie. He fell in love with Amanda over chess at the youth club and one day (no, not just one day: it was this day, the fourteenth day of May in 2004, the most important day of his life) Bertram asked her out on a date.

Amanda said yes, to his great surprise.

Amanda was pretty, in a girlish sort of way, the sort of way that turns to plain in older age. She was clever, witty, a little bit wise for one so young. She knew the way to Bertram's heart was love and ragtime music. Love was down to her, and she threw herself into falling in love with Bertram Wilson with the sort of brio that only an eighteen year old with ambition can muster. Fats Waller and his rhythm (1934-1936), imported from America and wrapped in silver paper decorated with hearts, supplied the source of Bertram's ragtime joy.

The two became an item.

'Will you marry me?' Bertram asked on the twenty-third of July 2005, in the balcony of the Whitby Pavilion. Below them, Michael Marra was singing a song about Frida Kahlo. It seemed so jaunty, so hasta la vista lovely that Bertram thought it the ideal backdrop for such a tender moment.

'Of course,' said Amanda. Her eyes shone. Her heart sang. Her hands trembled with anticipation. They set a date, a wasted date as we already know, but since they set it I may as well tell you that their marriage was to be at 2 o'clock on April 4th 2006 in the Nightingworth Church in Sussex.

(Another couple, Irene Thomas and Peter Gethsemene, will marry on that day, at that time, in that church, but they are not as well suited as Amanda and Bertram, and their marriage won't survive longer than a year.)

You're impatient for the end, which is a shame for Bertram. Don't you feel guilty, reading so fast, hastening his death in this unseemly way?

No, plainly not.

It was November 18th 2005, at 10.25 am when Bertram Wilson heard a knock on the door. 'I wonder who that is,' he said to himself. He paused Fats Waller in the middle of 'Ain't misbehavin'', apologised for such effrontery and took what was, though of course he didn't know it, his last walk to the door.

'Yes?' he said, surveying the man on the pavement. A curious man, sunken-eyed, grey-pallored, the sort of expression you see in someone who hasn't slept all night.

'I'm the author,' I said.

'I don't understand.'

'I know you don't, Bertram. You understand nothing but love and Amanda and ragtime music.'

'How do you know?'

'Because I made you that way.'

Bertram Wilson stared into my eyes. I stared into his. In unison, we started to cry, though he didn't know why.

'I'd have preferred it if you made me like Nirvana, to tell you the truth. All that bloody ragtime sounds the same after a while.'

I lowered my eyes, saddened. It's always a poignant moment when a character takes on a life of its own, but you can't let them get too big for their boots. This isn't Eastenders, after all.

Reader, I shot him.

Tom Conoboy

Red Faced Men

So you live in Paradise – Paradise, Ca. Your life is surely heaven, strolling the boardwalk to a soundtrack of Beach Boys and surf breaking gently on the shore.

There are palm trees, and blue skies, and golden, golden sand. The sun is sunnier than anywhere else on the planet, the water warmer, the girls more beautiful. And the men are called Lance, or Brad, or Josh and are golden haired, tan and lithe.

But you, you are not tan and lithe. You are dark and overweight, and the stress of your life has turned your face red till you look like you will explode.

You do not see palm trees, hear melodic surf. Even when you head to the beach, you stumble across a drive-by shooting, hear curses, hear your own curses, see nothing but pain, anger, pain.

When you go to the bar for a cool beer, a chair thrown by a Latino woman from a third floor window lands in your path and you step into a puddle left over from the solitary rainfall in weeks.

It is all too much.

At the bar you meet Richard and Dennis. Richard has lost his wife and kids and is losing his hair. Dennis is plain fat. You stare at the bar and your stress turns to sadness till the three of you are weeping silent fat tears into your Coors.

'Hey guys!' one of you says. 'Hey!'

This is the rallying cry, the call to the American inside you.

You drain your glasses, agree that all you need is a change of scenery, a hike in the woods maybe. You fix it for the weekend, return to your room, a little lighter, a spring in your step.

You look in the mirror and ignore the shot blood-vessels, the unhealthy tinge to your skin. 'I'll pass,' you say. 'I'm not so bad. I'm not.'

The next few days, more shit happens.

A blond haired skater runs over your foot (you are wearing sandals) and you curse and curse and turn redder and redder till a cop comes over and books you for a violation.

The skater looks on with disdain and pity.

Water from the solitary rainfall in weeks has been logged in your gutter, and when you have your head out the window to breathe in sea air, it finally gives, drenching you, leaving the aroma of decomposing leaves on your skin all day.

The weekend cannot come soon enough.

You guys take a train north to Pine Lodge. Plaid shirts, chinos and a stout backpack apiece suit your frame and your colouring better than your ironic Hawaiian shirts.

You feel more like a man already. You steal a look at the others and know they think the same too.

In the woods, the light is dappled, green. It tones down your skin, makes you look almost handsome. There is quiet, broken only by the tread of your boots on the soft leafy carpet. And birds, a few birds.

No Beach Boys. No surf. No curses. No

pain, already you know that here there is no pain.

You walk all day, resting against broad tree trunks to eat nuts and fruit from your packs. When daylight begins to fade, one of you says quietly, 'I suppose we should…'

Another one – you! – says 'Hell no.'

'Hell no, I won't go.'

Pretty soon the three of you are dancing around whooping and chanting 'Hell No! We won't go,' over and over till it IS too late to go.

So you climb into the yielding branches of a silver birch and make your bed there. You sleep like a baby, warm and secure.

In the morning you look at the faces of the other guys and know that you will all stay, without a word being spoken.

You climb birches, and swing down on their branches for the hell of it. You had forgotten what it is like to play, and now you know, you never want to stop.

By the fourth day, you are living in the high branches of redwoods. You look up and see sun; you look down and see green gold carpet. Up sun, down carpet. The animals are your friends. The world is your friend.

But you are weeping, the three of you, and you don't know whether it is because this is all too beautiful, or because you can hear a barking dog, the approach of rangers, come to find you, to prove that it cannot last.

Fleur Chapman

I Heart Pottery

Like me, my mother spends her life at a turntable. Yes folks, some people go potty when their marriage breaks down but not Susie Smith – she went pottery instead. And when she turns pots in the kitchen, I make tracks to my bedroom (to make tracks *in* my bedroom). There's a kind of sweet symmetry now that I think about it; or maybe there's something seriously wrong with a mother and son who watch things go round and round and round all day long.

If you catch her on a bad day she'll wax lyrical about how pottery was taken over by men in the third millennium because women had so many other things to do. So this is her way of showing that . . . she now has nothing else to do? I always get confused about that part. When Dad left she stopped doing all her usual stuff (including bathing for a brief time; she still never wears any slap). Then her friend Margot bought her a potter's wheel and it took off from there. Margot's into art as therapy. She's mad as a box of frogs and her house is full of homemade junk. Or maybe I'm just cynical.

For Christmas, Margot bought my mother a t-shirt that said 'I Heart Pottery'. She was wearing it the night I came downstairs and found her pedalling the empty wheel with her head cocked and tears rolling down her face.

'I don't know what to make next,' she said. I went over and put my arm around her; knelt down and held her foot still.

'Why don't you stop for a bit? You've made loads,' I said. She sniffed a bit and then shrugged me off, started pedalling again so I headed back upstairs. All night I lay there listening to the turning. I wanted to smash the thing to pieces. Bloody Margot.

We didn't make eye contact the next morning. Well, she might have been looking at me but I couldn't stomach looking at her. It's madness, just watching your life go round and round like that.

Around lunchtime she said: 'I'm just trying

to make sense of it all.' I didn't answer her. When I went up to my room that night there was something waiting for me on my own turntable. A mug. Looked like her best piece yet. She'd painted on it: The World Keeps Spinning Around.

Somewhere inside that potter is my mother. Now all I have to do is find a way to fire her up again.

Emily Gale

Mr Armstrong

Behold the duck! That's what Mr Armstrong used to say. And we'd all peer at the lake, hands up to our eyes, shielding the sun. I'd pray for sunny days because Mr Armstrong would call the register then troop us in for assembly, but we knew as soon as we got back to our classroom he'd get itchy feet and take us to the park. It was great being in 3PA. Everyone wanted to be in our class.

He'd lie on the grass with his hands behind his head and call our names and ask us to recite poems or test us on the names of flowers and trees. Now and then we'd practice our times tables, but not often.

When he died, they let us walk behind his coffin and as we went past the big gold gate of Vicky Park, they stopped and we sang 'All Things Bright and Beautiful'. Right there, out in the street in the middle of Bow. Twenty-eight kids singing their lungs out and looking over at the lake and wishing Mr Armstrong wasn't dead.

Janet Bradshaw

Red Traffic Lights

It's stop every time at the All Red Traffic Lights. The sisters take it in turns to sit in the tree house at the crossroad, watching for hours the empty, sandy roads. There's a handful of buildings, a child's hand, that is, round the crossroads. A café, a garage, a shop, three or four houses. About a half a kilometre to the north, there's a farm.

Just as they are nodding off, or just at a particularly engrossing part in their book, they hear the droning of a vehicle. They look up and see it. At least five minutes away. Time to clamber down the ladder, hot foot across to the garage and tell Mr Jenkins. Time for him to press the buttons to switch the lights on the traffic lights. Stop the traffic.

The van stops. Drew comes out, bucket and wash leather, wipes the window as the driver sits waiting for green. Waiting. They wind down the window.

'Hey, how longs this take? These lights?' They stare right and left, up the sandy road for miles. No traffic. 'It's a mighty strange place for traffic lights.'

In the café they are watching. Placing bets; how long before the driver puts their foot down and drives off.

Someone opens the café door and comes over with a coffee. 'Take a while sometimes, those lights. Want a drink while you wait? Or step inside, sir. We've a menu here worth spending some time over.'

They might look up, scratch their head. Puzzled, disbelieving. 'I don't think so. I gotta get on.'

'As you like, sir. But it's another coupla hours before the next little town. Nowhere between here and there. You might want to stop and refresh yourself. And maybe fill up your tank. And give the ol' jallopy a rest too.'

'I don't think so.'

'As you like. But we've got some mighty efficient traffic cops here. You go through them there lights at red they'll be after you. You might not see them, but you can bet that they be watching you. They'll be bringing you back here and you'll be answering questions and filling in forms the rest of the morning and into the afternoon. Not to mention any fines. It'd be quicker to wait, have yourself a rest and something to eat.'

Sometimes they were maddened and just drove off, quick as you like, without a doff of the hat or a good day. But often they agreed, moved the car over to the café and went in.

It started quiet, the trade in this little town, but it got a bit of a reputation and folks started driving that way on purpose, doing a detour to show their friends this strange place they'd discovered. The woman who ran the café got enough money to build a couple of rooms on the side for people who got stopped late in the afternoon. Two nights a week there was music, live, all performed by people who lived at the crossroads. The café was busy. In summer they put tables outside.

The local television station came, interviewed the people who got stuck there and the people who were making their livings from the drivers. The broadcast was seen by someone in the traffic section at the local government office. They sent someone down to check the lights.

The engineer arrived, stopped at the lights. He was tempted into the café. Then, the lights still being red, he went into the little store that had opened next door. Picked up a couple of books, and some local salmon to take back for his tea. Finally he ran a quick check on the lights. Went back and reported that they were a bit slow but all seemed in order, nothing to worry about.

So the lights at the crossroads carry on turning to red and staying at red, and drivers still drive that way so they can stop. And rest awhile. And talk and eat. If you go that way and look in the café you'll see the tables full, you'll hear the banter and laughter as the drivers wait for the lights to change.

Penny Aldred

What Brendan Done Today

The pub is heaving, Friday night, but in a corner, sat on his own, is Brendan. He's playing doms right enough, but not with anyone I can see. He's one set open on the table, and as I watch, he knocks. Can you knock when you're playing yourself?

He shoves the table away, grabs his glass and weaves across to the bar. And for the first time ever in the history of the world, his jacket shoulders are where his jacket shoulders ought to be. Brendan is wearing a suit.

'Do you not think you've had enough?' I hear Niamh say. 'Go home Brendan. It'll look better in the morning.'

'Will it?' he says, and for the first time ever in the history of the world, I watch him start to cry.

'Listen,' he says to Niamh through a face full of snot, 'you know what I done today?'

She shakes her head. She's heard it all before, but I know that's not true. She's never heard it from Brendan. None of us have. He's the gas man, the owld bugger, the one we all laugh at, with. This doesn't sit right. His suit does, mind. But this doesn't, this mood comin' off him.

'Brendan,' I say, sliding up to him and winking at the girl, 'will you take a drink wi' me?'

The girl nods, and I gather Brendan up and hoist him back to his doms.

'You're a good man so,' he says as he sweeps the table clean with a sleeve. 'A good man so.'

'What's up?' I say.

'Ah, nuthin',' he says, but I know for a fact it's a big 'nuthin''.

Niamh carries the drinks over on a tray, slides on the doms, drowns the pair of us in Murphy's. The poor child is gutted, and while I watch the cream slide down the front of Brendan's suit, some gobshite walks past, gives her elbow a nudge, and sends the other pint flyin'.

Brendan is up and he squares on the culprit. 'Some anybody everyself, are yer?' he says, sober now.

The gobshite folds. 'Ah no, Brendan,' he

says. 'It was an accident.'

'Some accident,' me and Brendan say, and Brendan nuts him. He might be a squit but he's a squit wi' muscle.

Niamh rounds on the gobshite. 'Out,' she says. 'Now.'

And with me and Brendan watching, he does just that, takes himself off and out through the door without a word.

Niamh reappears with a mop and a bucket.

'Leave that,' I tell her. 'I'll do it. Just bring the drinks.'

She sighs. 'It's not your job.'

'It's not yours, either,' I says to her. 'Honest. It'll be right. Just bring the drinks.'

While she's gone, I settle Brendan onto another table and swab the decks. Mary Poppins I ain't but I think I done a good enough job.

'So what happened?' I say to Brendan when I've finished.

He shrugs and reaches into his pocket, pulls out a plastic pouch. 'I scattered the Mrs,' he says, 'what's left of her.'

Zoe King

Whatever Will Be

My grandmother coughs on something she hasn't quite swallowed and I remember Bobby Spears from way back when as I slap her back. Her cough is thick with phlegm; his was dry and short, like a machine gun, but it takes me back just the same.

Like it was yesterday, only it wasn't. There has been a lot of water since then, and I have crossed many bridges.

I'm smiling, even as my grandmother's face bleeds purple.

It followed Bobby wherever he went. Some people bit their nails, others played with their hair. With Bobby it was that damn cough.

Rat-at-at-at.

Rat-at-at-at.

There was nothing in it, nothing at all. It was just a part of who he was.

You liked Bobby, so you learned to live with his idiosyncrasy. Hell, I only had to put up with it in the playground and summer holidays. His parents had the sharp end of that stick.

My grandmother sits up straight. She has dodged the bullet once again. I tell her to be more careful and she looks at me as if the worst thing in the world you can do is throw a life lesson at someone with twice as many years as you.

I sit down and wait for it to happen again, and think some more about Bobby as I do.

I wonder when the cancer visited him. I never noticed.

One day Bobby coughed himself right out of a game of hide-and-seek, and the next the doctor told him he had cancer. Twelve years old. They gave him six months to live, but that cancer ate away at him like he was its first meal, and it only gave him three. His funeral felt as much mine as his.

Now my grandmother looks at me as if she has something important to say but is waiting for me to ask, so I do. She smiles, toothless and tender, grabs my hand in hers and, as if she has been walking with me through my thoughts, says:

'Que sera.'

And, of course, she is right.

Brian Ross

Wearing Pink Naked

She wore pink. Her car was pink. She carried a pink handbag. She looked like a joke sometimes. But who was I to judge a pair of legs like that? No matter how pink the skirt was.

Don't get me wrong, she wasn't swathed in the colour, not all the time anyway. She didn't leave the house every day looking like a stick of bubble gum. Just sometimes. But there was something pink on her person every moment of the day. Even when naked. Showering, bathing, making love, she made sure there was a bellybutton stud or earring or scrunchie attached to her; something pink.

It didn't bother me. I don't have small hang-ups like that. It bothered her. The first time she didn't wear pink was at a funeral. Her mother's funeral. At this funeral, her father collapsed of a heart attack and croaked right there in the church. A year later, she wore no pink to a team diving competition, smashed her skull on the board and woke up in hospital two days later. The final time she didn't wear pink, the time that persuaded her, finally, that not wearing pink was, like, the worst thing in the world, was when she hit a dog with her car, late for work and hungover.

I actually found it kind of cute.

And she was no bimbo either. This was no *Clueless* girl, no *Legally Blonde* 3. She was just who she was. A girl - a woman - who wore pink.

'It's a confident colour,' she said on our first date. 'It takes a certain person to wear pink.'

'Sure,' I'd said, then concentrated on getting into her pink knickers.

And get in them I did. Hell, I even wore a pink condom when she asked. It wasn't just cute anymore; it was a full-on turn-on.

But then she suggested I, too, wear pink. She bought me a pink shirt for my birthday, pink socks on a whim, then at Christmas a pink watch with Minnie Mouse working her arms as hands. I'd not been happy at the last one.

'A joke,' she said, her eyes dead.

Furious at this assault on my masculinity, I told her, 'I'm never wearing pink.'

She cried that night in bed. Her warm back and buttocks against my stomach and thighs, I held her. I stroked her breasts, her stomach, felt for the stud in her naval. She pretended to be asleep. I asked her why pink. She stirred, said, 'Why not pink?'

I fell asleep, my fingers on this little pink stud, and when I awoke, somehow, she was gone.

I dressed in pink for her; my pink shirt, my pink socks. I did not wear my pink watch, but carried it in my pocket. I went to look for her. At her place, but it was empty, her clothes gone. At her friends' places, telling them, 'Let her know I'm wearing pink,' and they smiled at me and shut the door, each of them sad.

And so I wear pink. Even though I hate it. Every day, hopeful of finding her again. Pink, every day. No matter what.

Even when I'm naked.

Antony Davies

Bruce Robinson Broke my Heart

I finally spoke to the film director Bruce Robinson today. We were in the local Spar. It was quite a moment when I saw him walk in. People laugh at me for having a bit of a hero-worshipping thing with some people, but I can't help it. He lives not far from here and I have noticed him around. I say I've noticed him around; I suppose it's a bit more than that. I could tell you most of his movements over the past couple of years. I could tell you how many coats he owns (at least three, although it was the first time I had seen the sheepskin jacket he was wearing today), when he last had his hair cut (two months ago, at Sheila's), and the number of pints of local ale he had last weekend in the King's Arms.

I didn't tell him any of this. He doesn't know who I am. I have almost spoken to him on so many occasions I've lost count. I need my brain to keep track of the man. I don't have time for extraneous details about my own life.

So. We were in Spar. I was buying a bottle of wine, some tin foil and something or other.

He was buying twelve button mushrooms and a block of championship cheddar. I admired his choice of cheese. I was going to comment on it but I couldn't find the right moment and he went out of the shop. I cursed myself for yet again failing to muster the courage to speak to the man. 'Cursed' is too weak. A tide of unadulterated self-loathing washed through me. When he came back in to buy two bags of ready salted crisps and a bottle of 1998 Merlot I told myself, Robert, now is your chance. You absolutely have to talk to this man. I tapped him on the right shoulder of the sheepskin jacket.

'Bruce,' I said. 'I was wondering if you would like to embark on a correspondence that will be studied by film biographers in years to come?'

Bruce gave me a look that made me worry I had got the wrong man. I smiled.

'I'm a bit…' he muttered something and dodged out of the shop. I followed him.

'Bruce, I'm sorry about that, I was just trying to get your attention. The thing is, I'm trying to make my own films, and I don't really know what I'm doing, so I wondered if you could maybe give me a few tips? And then I was thinking we could write to each other about films and our lives and then the letters could be saved by our wives long after we're dead – of course, it won't matter to us then – but it's the principle of the thing, you know?'

By now Bruce had started walking more quickly. I had to jog to keep up. He was very fit for a man of his age. I was getting desperate.

I pointed to my long coat.

'Bruce, I'm wearing this coat because I want to look like Withnail. I look forward to winter so that I can wear it.'

'You sad bastard,' said Bruce.

I was not to be defeated. I had followed this man for months. I had seen him in the local pub with a TV gardener who lives round here. I had seen him come out of the bank, I had seen him park his car. This was important. This was my only chance.

'How's your book on Jack the Ripper going? Can I help with anything?'

'Look, what do you want from me? I'm very busy, my wife is expecting me home, I don't know who you are, I have work to do, and I'm running out of patience.'

This was not going as planned. Maybe he was having a bad day? I tried once again. 'I've read your interviews, I know that you like to vacuum while you write so that you can think of voices for your characters…and my wife's friend's sister is friends with your daughter, so we're practically related.'

'I'm going home. Please don't ever talk to me again.'

I knocked on his window. I was almost in tears.

'I've got your address from a teacher at my wife's school, maybe I could come and visit you some time?'

'You come near my house and I'm calling the police. Now piss off.' And he roared off in one of his three cars.

The rude bastard. I mean, what more could I have done? That's the last time I slavishly follow someone around for years and years.

Dave Prescott

The Farmer and the Loaf of Bread

At the end of this story, there's a farmer, standing with a woman in a black wedding dress. They stand on a cliff top, high above the waves, watching a bird build a nest out of nothing. The bird is white, with soft grey wings and a delicate head. It is perched on a ledge no wider than a man's hand and between its yellow feet is a single egg. It nudges it with its beak and the egg rolls slightly towards the sea, but it rolls back on itself, oval-shaped, and the woman, who had put her hand to her mouth as she watched, breathes out softly.

The man looks, follows her gaze, then takes her hand and they walk together towards the land, away from the sea.

But that is the end of the story, and before that we have to have an orange pumpkin, grown on a heap of warm manure, the pips scooped out and fed to the pigs, the flesh eaten hot, in pies. There has to be the naming of parts, a lover's song and a young boy who steals a loaf of bread that had been left to cool on a windowsill and who walks on, breaking off chunks and scattering crumbs for the sparrows.

The boy, of course, will become the lover and then the farmer, and it is the woman who baked the bread, but she did not know that it was him who had stolen it. And the time when the boy became a lover, when he learnt what warmth and dark and urgency meant, and the smell of hay and the taste of a woman's breast, that time for him was not the same time for the woman: for she was already married, was teaching her own children how to grow pumpkins from seed and where to pick blackberries, warmed by the sun.

So later, when the boy became the farmer and tasted the woman's bread again, but as a neighbour this time, as a guest, he looked across the rough table and saw that she knew. And although, somewhere, her eyes said that it was time, her body told him to wait, because the time of the eyes and the time of the body is not always the same and the boy-lover-farmer understood this too.

So now, they walk together back to the land, back to the farmhouse where she has baked a fresh loaf of bread for them to share, now that the wedding guests have gone. They will break it together, and then climb the stairs and it will feel like the first time, and the last, and all the spaces in between.

Katherine Pirnie.

Tom Brown's Spaceship

My son Tom doesn't believe in God. He doesn't believe in Buddha, Mohammed or Jesus either. Tom believes in Space (the final frontier). To Tom, heaven is a convoy of giant, invisible spaceships, chock full of souls and they're all out there somewhere, slipping through space, galloping through galaxies, unearthing new universes. I don't really mind that Tom worships at the church of Star Trek. In fact I'm quite jealous of his unquestioning faith. It's better to believe in something than nothing at all.

The last time we went to church (Christmas 2003; Tom was seven) he spent the entire service reading his new book 'Star Trek: The Language of Space'. When the service finally ended we queued to greet the vicar. I wished him a Merry Christmas and he limply shook my hand (do they all have handshakes like wet fishes?). Tom, my sweet boy, avoided the vicar's damp palm: instead, he gave the Vulcan salute and said “tich tor ang tesumur” (‘live long and prosper’). The vicar just smiled and said, ‘They’re so full of energy, aren’t they?’ Yes, yes, they were, and so was Tom, until 20 minutes later when he had a fit on the driveway as we piled out of the car. I carried his limp body through our front door.

There had been fits before. He had his first one at 18 months and I watched in horror as his small, plump body thrashed and writhed on the kitchen floor. We rushed him to A&E and the doctors checked him over. ‘Nothing to worry about,’ they said. ‘Fits are common in small children. Bring him back if it happens again.’ But it did happen again. It happened again when he was two years old, and then three. There was a temporary period of respite between four and six (and we quietly mouthed thank God) but they began again, with increasing regularity.

When Tom turned nine, he had five fits in four months and then the headaches began and the little floaters that appeared before his eyes. ‘They’re like little aliens, Mummy. Way cool!’ We took him back to the doctors and we prayed for ‘Nothing to worry about’ but we got

'We're very sorry.' We prayed for cures, for fixes, for miracles, for hope. We got 'There's nothing we can do. We're really very sorry.'

Tom didn't like the hospital. He didn't like the plain white sheets and the thin, flat pillows. He wanted his Star Trek duvet cover, his spaceship wallpaper and his wall to wall books. He wanted to watch the movies on repeat and stare up at his posters. We asked to take him home, said we had to take him home. I wanted to see him in his own room, as ruler of his little galactic empire, not as one small, too tiny boy, lost in a huge, white ward, tucked into a too white bed.

So we took him home and we tucked him in. We sat on the edge of the bed and watched as he read. We brought him medicine stained green with food dye to look like alien booze and we stroked his hair. We watched him grow pale and thin, and we screamed at God when Tom couldn't hear. We had the talk. *The* talk. The one about whether or not to tell him what was happening. We held each other and we cried. What was right? What was wrong? Could we live with whatever decision we made?

We wiped our eyes, learned the Vulcan salute, made cakes in the shape of planets, painted on smiles that must not fade…but Tom knew. He knew. I was spooning tomato soup into his mouth when he held up his hand. I paused, the spoon hovering between us like a silver shuttle rich with molten lava. He looked up at me with pale, grey eyes. Tired eyes.

'Am I going to die, Mummy? If I'm going to die I need a spaceship. Can you build me a spaceship, Mummy? Daddy could help.'

Tom doesn't believe in God. He doesn't believe in Buddha, Mohammed or Jesus either. Tom believes in Space (the final frontier) and he's going there soon. Going in his spaceship all silver and gold - cooking foil, Christmas stars, plumbing pipes and scaffolding poles. It's buttons and buzzers, levers and knobs. There's a picture of space at the end of the bed and a curtain of stars above his head.

Cally Taylor.

Four Feet Below

Every weekend, tourists gather at Lake Placid to feel something new. They take to the water, roam nearby hills, rest on the smooth waterside lawn, run their fingers over new-mown grass.

Happiness finds its own level, so a few contented souls splash into the Lake in brand-new stripy swimsuits, float on its warm surface all afternoon, bobbing around in the gentle current.

Those on the grass lie back, drowsy in a summer glow. The sun is shining, but it's more than that. They don't know why, but looking across at their friends they see beauty, ripe, calm and fresh. What is there to do but kick back and enjoy the sun on their skin, picnic on chocolate and champagne, indulge in a kiss or two?

A little way out from the shoreline, there are a dozen or so waders, chest-high in water. Their level is four feet below, not deep enough to drown (though part of them wishes it were so). They don't seem to make progress. The pressure is too much, the weight against their chests incredible. But they carry on their slow, watery trudge. They can see the far shore. It's not so distant, not really.

Up in the hills lovers stroll hand in hand, but above them are those consumed by a fierce, incandescent joy. These are foothills to a dark, dark grey mountain, razor sharp, slate grey, slippery when wet. Today there is sun, and lizards bask a while, fix a beady, unblinking gaze on the foolish climbers.

There is one man, Joe, scrabbling up fast, pursued by another, a hunter, graceful, assured, holding a knife between his teeth. Joe seduced the hunter's wife, because he wanted her, but more than that he wanted this moment, the harsh rock scraping his shins as he pulls himself higher, the noise of the hunter behind, closing, the pull of the summit above.

If Joe can make it, he will explode with joy. But the hunter, who is grateful too for the chase (it is what he does, what makes his life worthwhile) has him. They come together on a ledge, grapple wordlessly, then seem to embrace before dropping over the edge.

As they fall, they pass the others, feel for a second or two their gentle pleasure, their calm contentment. Walkers stop in their tracks, shocked by the dangerous rush of blood to their hearts. But it passes, and they carry on, smiling, humming childhood melodies.

The men fall down, deep down. They crash through the surface of the water, still locked in their weird embrace. They pass the wading, waterlogged pilgrims, then others, sad souls who trawl the lake bed, laden with diving gear, tight suits, heavy oxygen tanks.

Still falling, they reach a cave, full of people who tried and failed, touched glory and spat it out.

'You'll like it here,' they say gloomily. 'Make yourselves at home.'

Fleur Chapman

Mrs Murchison & Man From Vienna

I don't think I will ever forget the moment I opened the letter: You are invited to attend the engagement party for Dylan Dylan of Dylan, Dylan & Dylan who is to be betrothed to Mrs Daphne Murchison, widow of the former Mayor of Dodderbridge…

Oh, how low I was. I was sick as a parrot, grim as a little pink pig with a hairy tail that wouldn't curl, flat as a cowpat. I wasn't that happy either.

But Dylan Dylan would not have her. He could not have her. I loved Mrs Murchison, loved her. We were made for each other. We had been made for each other from the day I walked into that warehouse and stumbled on the team working on her unmentionables.

Oh those drawers!

Mrs Murchison's drawers were unbearable, unfathomable, unimaginable. It took nine tailors six weeks working overtime just to strengthen the gussets, the silk from four parachutes to provide the double-linings, but no, I didn't mind, oh, oh, oh, no! It was that very size, that girth, and that wonderful weight, with which I was besotted.

I tried everything. I sent secret poems.

Oh, Daphne, my darling, I love you almighty!
I wish my pyjamas, were next to your nightie.
Oh, don't be mistaken, please don't be misled.
I mean on the clothes-line, not on the bed.

But none of them worked. All that was left was to find a way to stop Dylan Dylan. I had to find a way to persuade him that he could not cope with the magnificent Daphne, my wondrous behemoth.

'Trust Me, I am a Counsellor,' I said quietly. We were in my rented offices. I was wearing the white coat, the pince-nez glasses, and I spoke with a cultured Austrian accent.

'Yes, this is zo, and to zatisfy vill require…'

He was nodding, a mixture of intense fear and rapture in one.

'Een Meel-wowkee, in US of A, America,

also.'

'Are you sure?'

'Zertain. Ziss way lies eternal pleas-ure. For zair is zee vurled expert in such matters.'

Dylan Dylan left the next morning. He was never to return. Apparently a street robbery went wrong, not far from the airport. Such a tragedy. Bullet between the eyes, no, never felt a thing.

*

'Ach zo, Mrs Murchison. Of course, you must face the possibility, that your be-troth-ed was, in zee fact of it, a leetle intimidated. Only a discerning man, and vun who is the bravest could be vurthy of your charms.'

'You think so?'

'I zink so, Ya.'

'Someone like you, Doctor WickDipper?'

'Ya. Precisely, Mrs Murchison.'

Alex Keegan

About the Competition

33 writers wrote 450 stories over the course of 17 hours in response to Internet prompts. Each story was completed within a single hour.

The writers paid to fund their own prizes.

Leaf chose their favourite stories and the three winners.

Thanks to all the writers and to organisers Alex Keegan and Lexie Fox.

This book was edited by:
Sam Burns
Lewis Huxley
Barrie Llewelyn
Kate Millard

Designed by:
Cecilia Morreau
Gavin Pugh

For more information about Leaf Books and our services, please visit our website:

www.leafbooks.co.uk

- Complete List of Leaf Books
- Writers' Biographies
- Readers' Forum
- Ebooks
- Audio Books
- MP3 Downloadable Books
- Stockists
- How to Submit a Story to Leaf
- Competitions
- Writers' Services
- Jobs with Leaf

The First Leaf Short Story Competition Winner

THE GREENGROCER'S APOSTROPHE

Can this be Tom's last love song for Linty? The small, strange evacuee, the wife who turned apples beautifully, the lost old woman with soft face, faded eyes...how can he bear to let her slip away alone?

Alexandra North

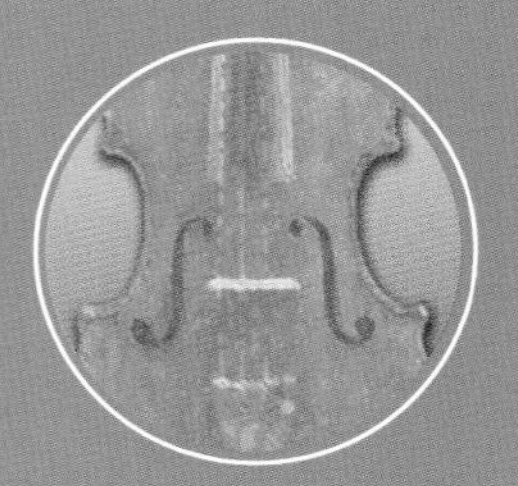

ADAGIO

Thomas can hear nothing, yet hears everything, listening with his eyes and with his heart. Helen, nervous in his company, hears everything, yet nothing. St. Cecilia and her guardians look down from the glass as Thomas and Helen embark on a journey that enlightens the mind and stirs the spirit.

Leaf

Saki

THE HOUNDS OF FATE

Slothful dilettante Martin Stoner is mistaken for the unspeakable ne'er-do-well Tom Prike. All the world, barring his adoptive uncle and dog, is against him. But Tom's grim life offers a refuge from destitution, the open sky and the muddy lanes that lead down to the sea.

Runner Up

Ghislaine Goff

THE GIFT

Guillaume de Rais, Principal Herald of France, is proud of his professional detachment. In medieval Europe, heralds are diplomats, the guardians of chivalry and umpires of battle – they ensure that the rules are kept. But when detachment becomes impossible, Guillaume discovers that he can no longer keep the rules.

Competitions and Submissions

The Leaf competition and submission calendar enables us to gather stories, non-fiction, poetry written by new and established writers in the UK and abroad.

Every entry or submission is read by at least two members of our readers' panel. The panel consists of book and story lovers who represent a wide selection of backgrounds and tastes. We are very proud of this selection procedure and believe it gives a fair chance to every writer who sends us their work.

Leaf Competitions Entry Form

Name________________________________

Address______________________________

____

____

Email ________________________________

Phone_______________________________

Competition Title ____________________

See Website for details of Competitions and Closing dates. www.leafbooks.co.uk

Title of Story/Piece/Poem

1.________________________________

2.________________________________

3.________________________________

4.________________________________

I enclose cheque, made payable to Leaf, for £________ (£5.00 for each story, £2.50 for each poem, and £10 for each critique).

Please send entries to:

Leaf, Gti Suite, Valleys Innovation Centre Abercynon, CF45 4SN.